INTERGALACTIC
P.S. 3

INTERGALACTIC
P.S. 3

MADELEINE L'ENGLE

SQUARE
FISH

FARRAR STRAUS GIROUX
NEW YORK

**SQUARE
FISH**

An imprint of Macmillan Publishing Group, LLC
175 Fifth Avenue, New York, NY 10010
mackids.com

Our books may be purchased in bulk for promotional, educational,
or business use. Please contact your local bookseller or the Macmillan
Corporate and Premium Sales Department at (800) 221-7945 ext. 5442
or by email at MacmillanSpecialMarkets@macmillan.com.

ISBN 978-1-250-30849-8 (paperback)   ISBN 978-0-374-31073-8 (ebook)
Library of Congress Control Number: 2017955156

Originally published in the United States by Farrar Straus Giroux
First Square Fish edition, 2019
Book designed by Elizabeth H. Clark
Square Fish logo designed by Filomena Tuosto

1 3 5 7 9 10 8 6 4 2

INTERGALACTIC P.S. 3

CHAPTER 1

It started at the dinner table.

It was the Tuesday night after Labor Day. Wind and rain beat about the house as they often seemed to do the night before the start of school.—*The weather feels the way I do about school beginning*, Meg Murry thought.

Charles Wallace Murry, the baby of the family, sat kicking his pajamaed feet against the rungs of his chair. "I suppose it will be all right," he said, cheerfully if not convincingly.

Nobody responded, and nobody was eating, both of which things spoke louder than words. Mrs. Murry had made her special spaghetti, which everybody loved;

she started to ask if anybody wanted seconds, then saw that nobody had finished firsts.

Mr. Murry's spectacles had slid down his nose, and he wore his absentminded-scientist expression, but he was not thinking about physics, or the present experiment he was con-

ducting in his lab, in which he was very close to producing a controlled molecule of anti-matter. This work was of the gravest importance to the United States, but at this moment his concern was entirely for his youngest son.

Meg, too, was thinking of Charles Wallace, rather than her own usual teenage rebellions. "I won't even be on the same school bus with Charles Wallace. I'm not going to be able to help at all."

Calvin O'Keefe, who spent more time at the Murrys' than in his overcrowded home where there were always dirty dishes in the sink and where nobody ever had quite enough to eat, was twirling long strands of spaghetti thoughtfully around his fork; and he had forgotten the Parmesan cheese. Calvin had no personal problems with school; he was captain of the basketball team and would be president of the senior class. It was because of Calvin's friendship and attention that Meg was beginning to think of herself as a possible person rather than the ugly duckling who would never grow up into a swan. Calvin, too, at this moment, was wholly concentrated on the little boy sitting across from him at the table. "Even the twins won't be on your bus, Charles. I wish we'd spent more of the summer teaching you judo."

The Murry twins, Sandy and Dennys, were off with their baseball team, despite the rain, and had eaten—with no loss of appetite—earlier. This was just as well, Meg thought; they'd only get mad at Charles Wallace for being different.

"Judo wouldn't do me any good," Charles Wallace said.

Calvin started, "I know you're against violence, but—"

"Even if I weren't, what good would judo do against a whole busload of kids?"

Mrs. Murry absentmindedly poured milk into Calvin's glass, which was almost full. "Perhaps we're just borrowing trouble when we assume that school will be difficult for Charles."

Calvin pushed his carroty hair back from his face with an impatient gesture; his worn blue sweater sleeves were much too short and exposed his strong wrists and forearms. "Let's face facts. Charles Wallace is going to get jumped on the first day, and some of the kids play rough. We already know that."

Charles Wallace leaned his elbows on the table, his chin in his hands. "You make me sound like some kind of freak, and a helpless one at that."

Calvin nodded grimly. "Facts number one and two."

Mr. Murry said, "Now wait a minute—"

"Father!" Meg cried. "Calvin's right. Charles Wallace is six years old and he's got an IQ so high it's outside testing limits, you told me that yourself. But everybody around here is used to

thinking he's not quite bright because he didn't talk till he was four. Even now he won't open his mouth unless he's around us."

"You know why," Charles Wallace said. He had grown during the summer, but his pajamas were inherited from the twins and were shabby and a little too big for him; instead of making him seem older, this made him look small and vulnerable.

"Because you know more about people than they want you to know."

"I don't *want* to know. That's why I don't talk. I'm never quite sure what they've told me in words and what they've told me in the other ways."

"There are times," Meg said, "when I wish you didn't always know what I'm thinking."

"You think very *loud*."

"Only to you. And that's the problem."

"Now, look, Meg," Mrs. Murry said, "your father and I have spent a number of wakeful nights discussing this. Charles Wallace looks like a perfectly normal six year old—"

"He's a mutant," Calvin said flatly.

Meg banged her fist on the table. "*I'm* not. And if school was awful for me, it's going to be even worse for Charles."

Mr. Murry pushed up his spectacles again. "It was largely your own fault, Meg. Calvin has managed."

"By pretending to conform." Calvin sounded bitter. "And by being bigger and stronger than the other kids. Charles is not."

"Don't you think," Mrs. Murry suggested, "that you may be underestimating Charles Wallace's adaptability?"

"I don't want him to adapt!" Meg shouted. "I want him to be Charles, special and different."

"Stop it, Meg," her father said. "We don't want Charles Wallace to stop being himself, either. That's not what adaptability means. And have you an alternate suggestion?"

The wind shook the house, and rain dashed wildly against the windows. Charles Wallace cocked his head to listen, gave a pleased laugh. "Yes, she does, and they're about to arrive."

"Charles! How did you know?"

"You told me."

"But I wasn't even sure myself that they'd come."

"Who?" Mrs. Murry asked. "What are you talking about?"

Again the house quivered against the wind's attack. Then there was a strange and sudden shimmer in the air, and the flames of the candles on the dining table stretched towards the ceiling. Meg jumped up. The shimmering seemed to solidify, then to separate into three shimmers, to quiver, assemble, gather color, and there, in the middle of the large kitchen-dining room, were three extraordinary beings.

CHAPTER 2

Charles Wallace clapped his hands joyfully. "The Mrs W! Meg, thank you for thinking of them!"

Now, if you do not already know Mrs Whatsit, Mrs Who, and Mrs Which, it is not easy to describe them. It's simpler to say the things they are not than the things they are. First of all, they are not witches, though it amuses Mrs Which to materialize in a somewhat witchlike form. This doesn't work quite as well as she thinks it does, because she finds it almost impossible to materialize completely; you can always see through her, and sometimes all that is visible is a shimmer topped by a peaked hat; and her voice sounds like the wind bumping into unexpected corners in a tunnel. Mrs Who is easily recognizable because she wears spectacles, round and twice as large and twice as thick as Meg's. She is a few billion years younger than Mrs Which, and can materialize with comparative ease, but has a hard time verbalizing; so when she is with earthlings she finds it easier to use quotations from earth philosophers and poets than to struggle for her own words and phrases. Mrs Whatsit is the youngest of the three, being not more than twice the age of our own solar system, so she is more apt at both materializing and verbalizing than Mrs Which and Mrs Who.

Meg and Charles Wallace and Calvin came to know the Mrs W when Mr. Murry, doing secret work for the government, was trapped on an alien planet and the children helped to rescue him. During the year since their return they had often talked about seeing the three strange and wonderful extraterrestrial beings again, and had come to think that this was not likely. "Except in time of extraordinary need," Meg had said. "I'm sure they'd come to us then."

Now she gave a slightly awed curtsy. "Thank you for—"

"Nno pprreambbles," Mrs Which said.

"I'm so sorry, my lambs!" Mrs Whatsit adjusted the multicolored assortment of shawls and scarves which she enjoyed wearing when on earth, and which made her look like a badly assembled bundle of missionary clothing. "We're in the midst of a particularly difficult assignment in Alpha Centauri, so we can't waste a second on preliminaries. Meg sent for us, and she was quite right to do so. For Charles Wallace to start first grade tomorrow will not do at all."

"How did you send for them, Meg?" Calvin asked, bowing in greeting to the three.

"I just thought and thought and thought. All last night I kept setting my alarm clock for every half hour, so I wouldn't fall asleep, and I called and called."

Mrs Whatsit nodded, so that the man's felt

hat, perched precariously atop her collection of shawls, almost fell off. "You did very well indeed, Meg, particularly since it is not one of your talents."

Mr. Murry had risen when the Mrs W arrived, and now he spoke rather stiffly. "Just what do you suggest? My wife and I have discussed the situation most carefully, and we feel that Charles Wallace must start school."

From Mrs Which came a shimmer of disapproval. "Charles knows more than is permissible in any first grader."

"We know that," Mrs. Murry said, "but we hope that if we don't make any issue of it at all, the children will accept him."

"The children!" Mrs Whatsit said. "Of course the children will accept him. We're not worrying about the children. The teacher is the problem. There's not one teacher in that school who is capable of accepting Charles Wallace as he is."

"Mr. Jenkins!" Meg clutched at her head in despair. "If Mr. Jenkins thinks *I'm* weird, Charles Wallace would really have him up a tree, and when Mr. Jenkins gets up a tree he gets mean."

"It won't do at all," Mrs Whatsit said. "We have come to take Charles Wallace away to school."

But Mr. Murry responded decisively and negatively. "We've already thought about that. Charles is far too young for boarding school, and why would the grownups there understand him any better than right here in the village school?"

Meg understood what her father did not.

She went to Mrs Whatsit and stood close to her. "You mean you're taking Charles Wallace *really* away—to a school that isn't on our planet, don't you? You're going to tesser him somewhere."

"No," Mr. Murry said flatly. "We've had enough tessering. The family is together at last. I won't have us separated again."

Mrs Who let out a gusty sigh and pushed at her spectacles in

a gesture reminiscent of Meg as well as Mr. Murry. *"Necesse est cum insanientibus furere, nisi solus relinqueris."*

Meg giggled.

Mr. Murry's shaggy scientist's hair bristled. "Mrs Who, I hardly think we are mad."

"Then pay attention to Meg," Mrs Whatsit said. "She is quite right. We are going to the Third Planet of the Teachers."

"No." Mrs. Murry put her arms about her small son.

Meg said, "Mother, Father, you don't understand. It's an interplanetary, intergalactic school. It's a big honor for Charles. You have to let him go."

Mrs Who's spectacles glinted. *"L'homme vit souvent avec lui-même, et il a besoin de vertu; il vit avec les autres, et il a besoin d'honneur.* The

Maxims of Chamfort. Man needs virtue because he must be often alone; he needs honor because he has to live with others."

Mrs. Murry tried not to hold Charles Wallace too closely. "Where is this—this interplanetary school?"

"On the planet Framoch, in the Mandrion solar system of the Veganuel galaxy," Mrs Whatsit said.

Mrs Which quivered with impatience and almost disappeared. "Tthere iss nno ttime fforr dissscusssion."

Meg ran around the table to her father. "Please, Father. You've tessered. You know there are things for Charles to learn that he can't learn here in first grade."

Mr. Murry exchanged glances with his wife. "Meg is right. We've always said that we would love our children with open hands. We can't hold Charles now."

Mrs. Murry took her arms from Charles, but said, "He's so young—and all alone—"

"Nnott allone," Mrs Which boomed. "Megg and Ccalvinn will go, tooo."

"*Me?*" Meg squeaked.

"You, petkin," Mrs Whatsit said.

"But I'm not special the way Charles is. I flunk exams and fight with my teachers—"

"You will learn not to fight with your teachers."

Meg rushed over to her mother, then back to her father, almost falling over her own feet in her excitement. "Please, let's go at once, before we have time to be too scared."

"Meglet," her father started, but Mrs Which interrupted.

"Shee iss rrightt. Therre iss nno ppointt in delayy."

Mr. Murry demurred, "But Meg doesn't tesser well—"

"I'll take care of her," Calvin said. "Mr. Murry, please, we'll learn important things to bring back."

"How do we know you'll ever come back? It's a very large universe, and Veganuel is half-way across it."

"Father," Meg said, "we brought *you* back, didn't we?"

"Yes, Meg, but we came very near to *not* getting back, even with all the help the Mrs W could give us. The powers of darkness are still there. If you think evil is going to let you alone this time just because we won last time, you don't know much about evil—and you don't. That's why I'm worried."

"But, Father, you've always said we can't refuse to do something just because we're scared . . . and I *am* scared, please, Father—"

Mrs. Murry drew Meg to her. "It will be all right once you're there. Send us a postcard." She laughed, but there were tears in her eyes. She turned to Calvin. "I'm glad you're going."

Mrs Which glimmered impatiently. "Nnoww. I ddo nnott llike llongg-drawwnn-outt ffarewwelllls."

"Wait—" Mr. Murry urged.

Mrs Who held up her hand. "Τοῖς νοι δικαίοις χω 6ραχὺς νικᾷ μέγαν. Sophocles. In a just cause, even weakness may win the day."

"You know that," Mrs Whatsit said to Mr. and Mrs. Murry. "Let them go, now. This is too important a trip for further discussion."

Mr. Murry held out his open hands.

And then Meg felt the wildness of tessering through absolute darkness, absolute bodilessness. In the split second between time and time she was whirled from feeling to non-feeling, matter to matterlessness. All the homely five senses vanished, to be replaced by an awareness past sense, which was wholly and acutely conscious during the trip through the intangible world of the strange spaces between matter.

It had all been so sudden that there had been no time for panic to build up inside her, and she knew that the Mrs W would never forsake her, never leave her in the absolute non-ness of the wrinkle between mass and time. When she felt her feet on solid ground again, she felt also the warm comfort of Mrs Whatsit's arms about her.

CHAPTER 3

They were standing on a lush, green hill. This World of the Teachers was a kaleidoscope of kindergarten colors, of warm scents and gusting breezes, completely different from any of the planets she had visited before. Around them were trees, flowers, birds, and a sense of spring as spring on earth hints at being but never fully realizes. Below them, where the hill leveled out into a flower-filled field, was a river, which, instead of flowing peacefully,

splashed and bounded with waterfalls and whirlpools. The sun was delightfully warm, but not hot.

The three Mrs W drew together. "You need no gifts from us this time," Mrs Whatsit said, "though you might remember some of the things you learned on Uriel and Camazotz and Ixchel. From you we expect the gifts of your learning. We will return for your graduation exercises." They were gone. Where the three forms had been was a clump of daisies dancing in the wind. Meg almost thought she saw the atoms of the air drawing in to fill the space where the Mrs W had stood.

"Charles—" Meg said. "You haven't said anything."

Charles Wallace's usually rosy face looked a little pale above the faded blue pajamas which he still wore. But he smiled at her and slipped his hand into hers. "Nobody gave me a chance. I would have liked to put on some clothes."

"But if you hadn't wanted to come, you'd have said something, wouldn't you?"

"It's all right, Meg," Charles said. "I'm a little scared; I don't think it's going to be easy here. But I'm probably less scared than I would have been going to school at home."

From behind them came shouts and laughter and singing, and a group came running up the hillside: a group of what? Children? They were children, yes, and some were even children who would have been recognized as children on earth. Then there were those who were familiar to Meg and Charles Wallace and Calvin, who were grateful to see small versions of the beautiful flying creatures from Uriel; of the strange, tentacled, eyeless beasts from Ixchel, horrifying to a human being at first sight but dearly loved now by the Murrys and Calvin. Then there were what must have been children of other planets, of other forms of life, some beautiful as the Uriel creatures, others even more terrible in appearance than the Ixchel beasts. Meg, recoiling in instinctive fear, remembered Aunt Beast, and that to judge by appearance is a mark of ignorance. Never-

theless, she held Charles Wallace's hand more tightly and moved a step closer to Calvin.

Then she gave an uncontrollable cry of horror.

If some of the "children" in the group were strange and horrible to look upon, the teacher following them was more horrible to Meg than any wild and unfamiliar life form could possibly be. But he was not strange. He was agonizingly familiar. He was Mr. Jenkins, the principal of the village school.

Charles Wallace said, "Hey!" in a startled way.

Calvin put his hand firmly on Meg's shoulder. "Wait. Maybe it's not—"

"But it is! It is! I'd know Mr. Jenkins if I found him under a pumpkin on the moon or in a cabbage patch on Venus."

"It couldn't be." Calvin's voice did not carry conviction.

"Why not?" Meg demanded. "If we could be tessered here, why couldn't he be, too?"

"Wait," Charles Wallace commanded in his most authoritative, small-boy manner.

"What for?" Meg wailed. "I want to go home. If he's here, let's get out."

Then, at a command from Mr. Jenkins, three of the children separated themselves from the group and came running—though with two of the children it could hardly be called running—towards Meg and Charles Wallace and Calvin. The first one, who was the closest to being a recognizable earth form (though it scampered, rather than ran), was not unlike a small, silver-grey mouse. Its ears were large and velvety, its whiskers unusually long, and its eyes shone like moonstones.

The second child was a mer-boy in reverse: it

had long, strong legs, six-toed feet in thonged sandals, and from the waist up it closely resembled a dolphin, with a great, grey, rather top-heavy marine creature's head, and a wide, amiable dolphin smile.

The third child was the strangest of the three, fierce and wild. Meg had the feeling that she never saw all of it at once. There seemed to be an extraordinary number of eyes: merry eyes, wise eyes, ferocious eyes, kitten eyes, dragon eyes. And wings—how many wings could one creature have?—wings in constant motion, covering and uncovering the eyes. It was the most savage-looking creature Meg had ever seen, and it made even Mr. Jenkins seem less disturbing.

The mouse-thing spoke, but not with either a mouse's squeak or a human voice. It

sounded like harp strings, and the long whiskers vibrated almost as though they were being
played. It did not give forth words, and yet it
was quite plain that it was saying something
like, "Hello, are you the new ones?"

CHAPTER 4

Calvin gave a grin of bravado. "I believe I'm supposed to say, 'Take me to your leader.'" He looked over his shoulder at the band of children disappearing over the hill, Mr. Jenkins with them.

An amused and slightly shocked laughter rippled through the three strange children. The mouse-thing, who seemed to be spokesman, said, "Oh, no, earthlings, you won't see the Teachers until you've been accepted."

"What's Mr. Jenkins doing here?" Meg asked.

But Charles Wallace cut impatiently across her. "What do you mean, accepted? Mrs Whatsit, Mrs Who, and Mrs Which brought us."

Mouse-thing shook its head, whiskers quivering, mooneyes gleaming. "Pull won't get you into Intergalactic P.S. 3. It's not who you know that matters, it's who you are, and whether or not you can pass the admissions test. Frankly, I have grave doubts, but Mr. Jenkins, as you so oddly call the Admissions Officer, has chosen us to be your partners, and we'll do the best we can for you. Of course it's his decision in the end, but he's made us promise to give you all the help we can."

"I might as well go home," Meg said flatly. "Mr. Jenkins will never willingly pass me in anything."

For once, Charles Wallace was not listening to her. He was not, she thought crossly, even caring. He stepped closer to the mer-thing with its friendly smile. Meg thought the alien children were all frightening, but at least Mouse-thing was smaller than she was, and managed to communicate in earth terms. She turned to it. "No wonder you have your doubts if Mr. Jenkins is the examiner. What happens if we fail?"

"You will be tessered back to your home planet."

Calvin announced, "If Meg doesn't pass, Charles and I will go home, too."

"What makes you think you have any more

chance of passing than she does?" Mouse-thing asked. "If I had to bet on one of you, she'd be the one."

"Oh, no," Meg protested. "Charles and Calvin both have much higher IQs than I have."

Again laughter rippled through the three children.

"How strange you are," Mouse-thing said. "You can't measure anything important by earth tests. How can your IQ nonsense measure poetry or music or love?"

Charles Wallace suddenly looked not nearly old enough for first grade anywhere. "It can't. And I only know the measurable things. I haven't had time to learn anything else."

Meg flashed to his defense. "You love me, and you know when I'm upset, and it matters to you. That can't be measured."

"It will do for a start," Mouse-thing said. "Let's get going. We only have a parsec before I have to make my preliminary report. And I can see I have a great deal to teach you."

Meg could feel Charles Wallace bristling. He had let down his defenses and now, she thought, he was regretting it. "It's not my fault I'm only six. I bet when I'm a billion years old I'll have learned a few things to teach *you*!"

Mouse-thing's whiskers twitched. "Age is immaterial. I was only born yesterday."

"Then what are you doing here? When did *you* pass the entrance examinations?"

"I really don't have to." Mouse-thing's ears fluttered airily. "It's only a form for me. There's only one of us born every thousand or so years, and we come here automatically. My tree hasn't had an offspring for seventeen hundred years. Of course it will take me twice that long to become full-grown myself, and this is only my second phase."

"You're going to tell us about your first phase whether we want you to or not," Meg said in her most ungracious manner. "So go ahead."

The many-eyed, many-winged creature gave a series of ripples which might have been either amusement or annoyance. The upside-down mer-boy crossed its legs and sat on the lush green grass, placid smile broadening.

Mouse-thing reacted only by an intensified quiver of whiskers. "Yesterday morning I was still contained inside the single golden fruit hanging from my tree. At noon it fell and burst open, and there was I, newly hatched. I was then podded and flown to the Veganuel galaxy and tessered here. This morning I flung off my pod, and *me voilà*! I am called Sporos, *not* Mouse-thing, by the way. When I finish the course I will be cowled and sleep for an eon, and then I'll send a small green shoot up out of my cocoon and start growing into a deciduous spore-reproducing, fruit-bearing conifer."

Charles Wallace looked horrified. "You're mad. My father is a physicist and my mother a biologist. You're not possible."

"Neither are you," Sporos replied indignantly. "Nothing important is. Come on, let's go, Charles. It's my bad fortune to have you assigned as my partner. Follow me." It scampered down the hill and into the field where it was immediately lost in the high, green grasses.

Charles Wallace said, "Meg—"

"You'd better go, Charles—"

"But you might need me—" he said anxiously. His extremely prickly pride would not allow him to say, "*I* need *you.*"

Meg said, "If I need you, I'll call. You'll hear me. You always do."

"Will we all be together, maybe, for meals?" Charles asked. He looked at the mer-boy and the multi-eyed-and-winged creature.

Mer-boy had taken off his sandals and was plucking blades of grass with his long, prehensile toes. The ferocious-looking child appeared to be asleep; its many wings were folded over its eyes. A small plume of smoke rose from somewhere within it.

"Go on, Charles," Calvin said. "Maybe this is part of the test."

Meg gave him a push. "Don't say goodbye. Just go."

Without a word, without looking back, Charles ran down the hill and into the field. As he reached it, the grass seemed to stretch up until it was taller than the little boy, and he disappeared into its green depths.

CHAPTER 5

The upside-down mer-boy turned its great grin on Calvin. With its toes it held a long, broad blade of grass to its mouth and blew. A sound came from it, not the shrill whistle a human being makes when blowing against a blade of grass, but a low humming. Meg closed her eyes and listened. She understood something about *partners*, and stepped in relief towards the mer-child, then realized in disappointment that it was telling Calvin that they were partners, and inviting him to go swimming.

Calvin, too, understood. "But I don't have a bathing suit."

Through the blade of grass the mer-child laughed, and Meg understood it to say something like, "You don't need a bathing suit here. We're all quite used to everybody looking different from everybody else, and nobody pays any attention after the first few moments."

"Meg," Calvin said, "I don't like to leave you."

"I'll be all right," Meg said stiffly.

The ferocious creature raised one of its wings in what seemed to be a yawn, and folded it again. A small tongue of flame flickered up through the smoke.

The mer-child blew against the grass

again. Meg translated something like, "Can't you call home if you need anything?" and then a horrified, "Oh, my goodness, I don't see how anybody as ignorant as you three seem to be can possibly manage. Do you mean on your earth you never communicate with other planets? You mean your planet revolves about all alone in space? Aren't you terribly *lonely*?"

"Maybe we are, a little," Calvin acknowledged. "But it's a very beautiful planet."

"That," said Mer-boy, "is probably a matter of opinion, and opinions aren't going to help you pass the test. I'd better see what time it is."

"How do you tell?" Calvin asked curiously.

"Sporos tells by the leaves, of course, and I tell by the way the water feels. Your schools can't be very good if you don't know how to tell time, and if you have to go to school on your own planet."

"I *do* know how to tell time. I tell by my watch."

"What's a watch?"

Calvin extended his wrist.

"That's a funny thing," Mer-child said. "Does it just work for your time, or for time in general?"

"Just for our time, I guess."

"You mean, if you wanted to know what kind of time is told on another planet, it wouldn't show you?"

"No." Calvin said. "And it's only the right time for a certain section of latitude and longitude on our own planet. But that's all we need for practical purposes. It's like geome-

try," he added rather pompously. "Euclidean geometry doesn't work when you get into Einstein's theories, but it's fine for use in everyday life. I mean, like a table surface being flat and solid. It really isn't, but when you want to eat dinner, it has to be."

"*My*, how confused everything must be on your planet. Come on, we'd better get into the water, because I have to ask time to stretch for us. There's too much to teach you otherwise."

Meg felt a pang of absolute panic. "My partner—"

Mer-child again blew against the grass. "*Somebody* has to be the cherubim's partner."

"The *cherubim*!"

"What did you think it was? Come on, Calvin, let's go."

"Meg—"

The blade of grass was blown upon so impatiently that it let out a raucous blast.

"Go on," Meg said. "He's not my idea of a cherubim, but he can't be any worse than Mr. Jenkins."

CHAPTER 6

Calvin followed Mer-child, running swiftly towards the river, and Meg was left with the— cherubim?! She felt utterly abandoned and forlorn. Somehow she had expected Calvin to protest a little more, to refuse to leave her alone with this fire-spouting beast.

Flame spurted skywards as she thought this, followed by billows of smoke; the great wings raised and spread and she felt herself looked at by all the eyes. When the wild cherubim-child spoke, it was directly into her mind. "I suppose you think I ought to be a golden-haired baby-face with two useless little wings and no body?"

Meg sighed. "It might be simpler if you were."

Two of the wings crossed and uncrossed. "I don't know what I've done that I should have you assigned to me. I have a hard enough job as it is. I really don't feel like coming back to school at all at my age."

"How old are you?" Meg asked.

"Age, for a cherubim, is immaterial. It's only for time-bound creatures that it even exists. I am, in cherubic terms, still a child, and that's all you need to know."

Meg tossed her head. "If you're going to be rude to me we might as well call it quits right now. Just get someone to tesser me back to earth and you'll be rid of me."

The cherubim thought a number of unspeakable things at her. "If you have been

assigned to me, I
suppose you are some
kind of a Namer, too, even if a primitive one."

"A what?"

"A Namer. What I'm at school again for is
to memorize the names of the stars."

"Which stars?"

"All of them."

"You mean *all* the stars, in *all* the galaxies?"

"Yes. If he calls for one of them, someone
has to know which one he means. Anyhow,
they like it; there aren't many who know them
all by name, and if your name isn't known,
then it's a very lonely feeling."

"Do you know my name?" Meg asked.

"Of course. Margaret.
Meg."

"Do you have a name? Or am I supposed to address you as Cherubim?"

"Προγινώσκεις: Proginoskes."

Meg sighed. "All right. I'll try to remember. Cherubim would be easier even if you don't look like one."

"I do. I look precisely like a cherubim. And don't get any ideas about calling me Cherry, or Cheery, or Bimmy."

Meg looked embarrassed. "All right. Pro—Progo—Proginoskes. What are we supposed to *do*?"

Proginoskes waved all its wings, which, Meg realized, was more or less its way of expressing, "I haven't the faintest idea."

She asked, "Am I supposed to learn the names of all the stars, too?" It was an appalling thought.

"Good galaxy no! It's got to be something

to do with your own planet." All the wings were drawn together, the eyes closed. Small puffs of smoke rose. "I think what you're supposed to do is to help humanoids feel more human."

"What's that supposed to mean?"

"Who makes you feel most *you*?"

"My parents. And Charles Wallace and Calvin. At least they make me not mind being me."

"And who makes you feel least you?"

Meg looked across the cherubim and saw Mr. Jenkins strolling towards them. "Mr. Jenkins."

"Who's he?"

"He's right there, behind you."

The cherubim shifted wings; eyes opened and shut. "Earthling, you only have two eyes. How can you see something I don't see?"

"Not something. Someone. Mr. Jenkins."

"What are you talking about?"

"Mr. Jenkins. The principal of our school."

"Earth-child, what are you talking about?"

"He's right *behind* you," Meg said. "And I want to know what he's doing here!"

All Proginoskes's eyes opened wide: it was a horrifying sight. They closed, very tightly, then opened again. "Earthling, there is nobody there."

At this point Proginoskes was completely blotting Mr. Jenkins from Meg's vision. She peered around one of the wings. The cherubim was right. There was nobody there. "But he *was* there."

"I don't like this. I don't like it at all."

Meg said anxiously, "Proginoskes, is something wrong?"

The cherubim rearranged all its wings. "I don't know. I feel distinctly uncomfortable."

"Why?"

"It was the teacher, and it wasn't the teacher—"

"What do you mean?"

All of the eyes were covered with wings. The great creature moved with incredible grace, and the movement of the wings reminded Meg of a great actress using a fan to express a combination of charm and confusion and a degree of shyness. The words which Proginoskes sent into her mind were, she was quite sure: "What will happen if I fail the examination?"

"You mean if *I* fail, don't you?"

Again came the fan gesture. "No, no. If *I* fail."

"But I thought you were supposed to be helping me?"

"We're helping each other. Didn't you realize? That's why we're partners."

"But Mouse-thing—Sporos—I thought he said—"

"He did. Pride, that's what they're apt to flunk out on, the Ancient Trees. There are so few of them, they're apt to think of themselves as being more special than anybody else."

"You mean he really will be a tree?"

"If he survives," the cherubim said grimly.

Meg felt cold. "But won't he?"

The cherubim shrugged its wings.

"But he's my little brother's partner."

"Let us hope that your little brother has his feet firmly on the ground. How's his pride?"

"It's a problem," Meg said, "but he does know that now, because it got him into terrible trouble on Camazotz."

The cherubim quivered. "That's a dark planet."

"Yes," Meg said. "It was horrible."

Meg felt the cherubim anxiously probing

into her mind. "Your planet—tell me—is it dark?"

"No," Meg said. "It's shadowed, but it isn't dark. At least not yet."

"But you have wars? People fighting? Killing each other?"

"Yes."

"And children going hungry?"

"Yes."

"And there's—there's hate?"

"Yes."

The cherubim pulled all its wings about itself in a protective gesture. Now it reminded Meg not of a great lady using a fan, but of an ostrich. Small jets of flame and smoke came out from under the wings. Meg could feel it thinking grumpily—*They told me it was going to be difficult. . . . Why couldn't they have sent me off some place quiet to memorize the stars? . . . Why not I.G.P.S. 1 or 2 or any place else? Or if I had to come here why couldn't I have had another partner? I'm too young, I'm scared of shadowed planets, what kind of a star has it got anyhow . . . ?*

Mr. Jenkins stepped out from behind the cherubim. "Why, Meg, how very nice to see you here!"

CHAPTER 7

Meg took an involuntary step backwards and ran her tongue nervously over the sharp line of her braces. Mr. Jenkins looked exactly as he did at school. He wore a dark business suit, and no matter how often it was brushed there was always a small snowfall of dandruff on the shoulders. His salt-and-pepper hair was cut very short, and he had an equally short mustache making a rough bristle on his upper lip. His eyes were a muddy brown behind bifocals. He was neither short nor tall, fat nor thin, and whenever Meg saw him she responded like a porcupine throwing out quills.

"Meg, don't you know me?"

She whispered, "Mr. Jenkins—"

The cherubim peered with a few of its eyes out from under one wing. For some reason he reminded Meg of Charles Wallace. She felt him probing, gently now, into her mind, in much the same way her brother did.

"Meg," Mr. Jenkins said, "I'm afraid I've always misunderstood you. Won't you please accept my apologies?"

"You can't be here, Mr. Jenkins." Her voice trembled. "It isn't possible."

"Why not? If you're here, why shouldn't I be?"

"But this is a school for *children*."

"Precisely. And I've been sent to help you. You know you're going to find it difficult to pass the examination by yourself."

"Pro—Progo—*Cherubim*!" Meg cried. "Who do you see?"

The wings shifted. More eyes opened and shut. "I think I only see what you think you see—it's an earth form. It makes me understand that your planet is indeed shadowed—"

"Then it probably *is* Mr. Jenkins."

"Meg, do, please, try to calm down." Mr. Jenkins used the reasonable voice with which he always started out when Meg was sent to his office. "I have only been sent here to Framoch to help you. It is in earth's interests to have you pass this examination."

"It is indeed," said Mr. Jenkins, and Mr. Jenkins strolled out from behind the cherubim. Another Mr. Jenkins. Mr. Jenkins Number Two bowed to Mr. Jenkins Number One. "You've had your little game. Hadn't you better be going?"

Meg backed right into Proginoskes, who opened one of its wings and pulled her close. She could feel a tremendous, wild heartbeat, a frightened heartbeat, thundering in her ears.

"We're Namers," she heard through the racing of the heart. "We're Namers. What is their Name?"

"Mr. Jenkins."

"No, no. This is the test, Meg. We have to give them the right name. We have to know."

Meg looked at the two men who stood glaring at each other. "Progo, you can feel in to me. Can't you feel in to them?"

"You're *you*," the cherubim told her. "I

don't know who they are. You're the one who knows the prototype."

"The what?"

"The real one. The only Mr. Jenkins who is Mr. Jenkins. Look—"

Meg tried to follow the cherubic eyes, all of which were fully open. Behind the ferocious-looking creature, calmly mounting the hill towards them, was a third Mr. Jenkins. He raised one hand in greeting, not to Meg or Proginoskes, but to the other Mr. Jenkinses. "Leave the children alone for a few minutes," Mr. Jenkins Number Three said.

The three Mr. Jenkinses walked past Meg and Proginoskes and went down the other side of the hill.

"We must think, we must think." Proginoskes sent up small spurts of smoke.

Meg sat down on the grass, still held within the strength of the cherubim's wings. The great beast seemed far less strange to her than the three school principals. "If you really are a cherubim—"

There was a great and smoking surge of indignation all around her.

She hit the palm of her hand sharply against one of its pinions. "Wait. Shut up and listen. You told me to think and I've thought."

"You don't have to think out loud. You're deafening me."

"If I'm going to think, I'm going to talk to you."

"You mean it's easier for you to put it all into spoken earth-words?"

"Yes. Please, Progo."

"All right. It means I have to think back at you in earth-words, too. What a bore."

Meg shouted, "This isn't any time for boredom!"

The wings were raised as though to cover invisible ears. "I'm just trying to be brave."

"Listen, Progo. Listen. Cherubim have come to my planet before. I think you've helped us fight the Dark Shadow."

"All I want to do," Proginoskes repeated, "is go some place quiet and memorize the stars . . ."

"Progo! You said we were Namers."

"I've told you and told you—"

"Yes, but I still don't know: what *is* a Namer?"

"I've *told* you. It's—what's your earth-word? It's a case of identity. You're a shadowed planet, and that means that people don't know their own names. They don't know who they are. A Namer makes persons be themselves."

"How?"

"You've got a funny earth-word, and nobody knows what it means: if I say it you'll just misunderstand."

"You *have* to say it."

"It's a four-letter word. Aren't four-letter words the bad ones on your planet?"

"Yes, but which one? Look, don't be embarrassed. I've seen all the four-letter words on the walls of the washroom at school."

"Love, then. That's how you make persons know who they are. You've got a lot of it, Meg, but you don't know what to do with it. If you don't fail the exam you'll be taught—oh, some of the things I was taught my first year at school. I had to pass a billion exams before I could qualify as a Star Namer. But you're a human person, and it's different with you. I keep forgetting that. Am I lovable? To you?" All about Meg eyes opened and shut; wings shifted; a small flame burned her hand and was rapidly withdrawn; smoke choked her.

And she wanted to put her arms around Proginoskes as she would Charles Wallace. "Very."

"But not the way you feel about that skinny Calvin? Meg, don't withdraw!"

"That's different."

"I thought so. That's the confusing kind. Not the kind you have to have in order to name Mr. Jenkins."

"But he's already named."

"Not by you."

"I hate Mr. Jenkins."

"Meg, it's the test. You have to name the real Mr. Jenkins, and I have to help you. If you fail, I fail, too."

CHAPTER 8

What would happen?"

"You'd be tessered back to earth. You know that."

"And you?"

"I will be given a choice. I can go with the others—"

"What others?"

"The Planet Darkeners. The dragons; the worms; the ones who made war in heaven.

That's what most of those who fail choose to do."

"Or—"

"I can choose to not myself."

"To what?"

"To *not*. Not be."

"No—no—"

"But that's the choice. To go with the others or to not myself."

"This not-business: does it last forever?"

"Nobody knows. Nobody will know till the end of time."

"Charles!" Meg called loudly. "Charles Wallace!"

"Leave him alone," Proginoskes said faintly. "He has his own test to pass. We have to do it with the partners who are chosen for us."

"But he said to call him."

"You mustn't. He'll come. And he won't be able to help you and it might make him and Sporos fail. Every time anyone fails the test here, it's a victory for the Dark Shadow. It will make it even harder for your own planet."

Meg stamped, cried loudly and angrily, "This is too much responsibility! I'm still only a child! I didn't ask to come here!"

"Didn't you?"

"Of course not."

"I thought you called for the Mrs W."

"Because of Charles."

"When you call for creatures like the Mrs W you can't specify. If you call them, and they come, then you do whatever is next."

Over the crest of the hill strolled Mr. Jenkins. Only one Mr. Jenkins. Which one? There was no telling them apart—

"Progo," Meg cried, "if I fail, all that happens to me is getting tessered home?"

"If you can call it *all*," Proginoskes said. "There would be rejoicing in hell. But perhaps you don't believe in hell?"

Meg pushed this aside. "And you—"

"I told you. I'd have to choose to not myself, or—"

"Mr. Jenkins!" Meg said. "Please come here."

"Are you naming me?" Mr. Jenkins Number One asked.

"No. Wait. I have to ask you some questions."

"It is not allowed."

"I don't care whether it's allowed or not. If I don't ask you some questions how can I know whether or not it's you? What is the name of the school where you're principal? What state is it in, and what township?"

Proginoskes nudged her with one of its wings. "Don't waste time on questions like that. They all know the answers."

Meg went up to Mr. Jenkins. Checked his shoulders. There was the dandruff. She went closer: smelled. Yes, he had the Mr. Jenkins smell of old hair cream and what she always thought of as rancid deodorant. But all three could do that much; it was not going to be that easy.

He looked at her coldly in the usual way, down one side of his nose. "It has been most inconvenient for me to be brought here like this, just at the beginning of school, when I am already overworked. It seems to me I have had to spend more time with you than with any other student in school. It is certainly my misfortune. I have suggested to your parents that they send you elsewhere for my peace of mind, if not yours, but they seem to think that I have something to teach you."

This was Mr. Jenkins. He had played upon this speech with infinite variations almost every time she was sent to his office.

Now he said, "It is certainly in my interests to have you pass this test. If you fail, I'll just have you back in school again."

"You can say that again." Mr. Jenkins Number Two strolled over the hill. "My life will be a great deal easier this semester if we can just manage to pass you. Now, Meg, if you will just for *once* in your life do it *our* way, not yours . . . I understand that you're basically quite bright in mathematics. If you would simply stop approaching each homework assignment as though you were Einstein and had to solve the problems of the universe, and would follow one or two basic rules, you— and I—would have a great deal less trouble."

This, too, was Mr. Jenkins.

The cherubim shifted uneasily.

"Meg, I urge you," Mr. Jenkins Number Two said, "name me and let us have done with all this nonsense. I am Mr. Jenkins, as you well know. Stop trying to do things your own way."

CHAPTER 9

Meg," she felt Proginoskes probing wildly. "When have you been most *you*, the very most *you*?"

She closed her eyes. She remembered the first afternoon Calvin had come to the Murrys' for dinner. Calvin was generally a good student, but he was better with words than with numbers, and Meg had helped him with his math homework. She had concentrated wholly on Calvin and what he was doing, and she had felt completely herself.

"How is that going to help?" she asked the cherubim.

"Think again."

She remembered, unwillingly, the horrible moment on Camazotz when she had almost been pulled into the great, naked brain which ruled the planet. Charles Wallace had been drawn under its domination, and she had freed him purely through the force of the love which Mrs Whatsit had given her, and while she had been standing there, literally throwing her love at the imprisoned little boy, she had been wholly herself.

"But I can't love Mr. Jenkins!" she cried.

"You love me."

"But, Progo, you're so awful you're lovable."

"So is he. And you have to name him."

"Meg," Mr. Jenkins said, "stop panicking and listen to me." It was the third Mr. Jenkins and he had just appeared. The three men stood side by side, identical, grey, dour, unperceptive, overworked: unlovable.

"Meg," Mr. Jenkins Number Three said, "do you remember when you first tessered?"

"Who could forget?"

"If you will notice, I am the only Mr. Jenkins to remark upon this phenomenon."

Mr. Jenkins Number One waved this aside.

Mr. Jenkins Number Two said, "It is imperative that we stick to essentials. Tessering is, at this point, peripheral." Mr. Jenkins on earth was very fond of sticking to essentials.

Mr. Jenkins Number Three said, "Meg, did tessering make a difference in you? Has anything ever been the same since you first left earth?"

"No."

"It will never be the same for me, either. It was a frightening experience. And an ennobling one. You will not be the same girl I have had trouble with before. And I will not be the same, either. It has made me see many things differently. I understand your point of view much better than I did before. I think we were wrong to try to make you take all the regular courses at school. You *are* special, and we have made a great mistake not to realize this and treat you specially. I believe you and I had a—shall we call it a run-in?—over the imports of Nicaragua, which you were supposed to learn for one of your Social Studies classes. You were quite right when you insisted that it was useless for you to learn the imports and exports of Nicaragua. We will let you concentrate on numbers from now on, and not only that, if your methods of solving an equation differ from ours, we will realize, at last, that this is because you have been taught by an eminent physicist father. I am really sorry for all the needless pain you have been caused, Meg. And I can assure you that if you name me, you will find school a pleasanter place."

Meg looked at the three men: Mr. Jenkins, Numbers One, Two, and Three. "It's like a game on television," she said.

Mr. Jenkins Number Two looked down his nose. "It is not a game. The stakes are much too high. Do not be deluded by vain promises. You must be aware that he doesn't mean a word of it. He is not Mr. Jenkins. I am. Name me."

"If I name you," Meg said, "how will you treat me in school?"

"With concern. I will make every effort to

understand you, as I always have. But I will be realistic about it. We will give you all due consideration, which perhaps we have not done before, but we cannot turn the school upside down for one student. But I think you will find things less difficult than you have until now, even if only because you have tessered, as the impostor pointed out. If you will name me, as of course you must, since I *am* Mr. Jenkins, you will find that in the long run truth pays off."

Meg looked questioningly at Mr. Jenkins Number One. He gave a small, annoyed, Mr. Jenkins shrug. "I really do not foresee much change in our relationship in the future. Why interplanetary travel should be thought of as a solution to all earth problems I do not understand. We have sent men to the moon and we are none the better for it. Why sending you a few billion miles across space should improve you any, I fail to see."

Mr. Jenkins Number Three said, "It is quite obvious that he has never tessered. As the impostor now called Two remarked, I have, and I know the difference it makes. Don't be foolish, child. Think. And name me."

Meg turned her back on the three men. "They've switched. Mr. Jenkins Three, now, was Mr. Jenkins Two, before."

CHAPTER 10

Proginoskes looked at her with a series of its eyes, one by one. "That is immaterial. It's *now* that counts."

"Progo, if I don't name right—"

Progo flung several wings heavenwards.

"If I fail, what will you do?"

"I told you."

"No, you didn't."

"I did, too! I have to choose—"

"That's not telling me. I want to know which way you're going to choose."

Proginoskes went through a series of what seemed major upheavals. "Meg, there isn't much time. You can't take forever. You have to name one of them."

"Give me a hint—"

"He's right. It isn't a game."

"But you're my partner. Do you know which Mr. Jenkins is the real one?"

"Of course I don't. I've never seen any of them before."

"Am I supposed to feel love for the right one?"

Proginoskes opened its eyes very wide. "What a strange idea. Love isn't a *feeling*. If it were, I wouldn't be able to love. Cherubim don't have feelings."

"But—"

"Love isn't how you feel. It's what you do. I've never had a feeling in my life. As a matter of fact, I only matter with earth people."

"Progo, you matter to me."

Proginoskes let out several puffs. "That's not what I meant. I meant that cherubim only *matter* with earth people. Maybe you'd call it materializing. Most of the time we're winds, or flames of fire."

"Then, if you become visible only for us, why do you have to look so terrifying?"

"Because when we matter, this is how we come out. When you got mattered, you didn't choose to look the way you do, did you?"

"I certainly did not. I'd have chosen quite differently. I'd have chosen to be beautiful— oh, I see! You're not like the Mrs W, doing it the way you want to, just for fun?"

Proginoskes held three of its wings over

most of its eyes. "I am a cherubim, and when a cherubim becomes flesh, this is how."

Meg knelt in front of the great, frightening, and strangely beautiful creature. "Progo, I feel. I can't think without feeling. If you matter to me, then what you decide to do if I fail matters."

"I don't see why."

She scrambled to her feet and shouted, "Because if you decide to turn into a worm or a dragon or whatever, and work for the darkness, I don't care whether I name right or not! It just doesn't matter to me!"

Proginoskes probed into her mind thoughtfully. "I don't understand your feelings. I'm trying, but I don't. It must be extremely unpleasant to have feelings."

One of the Mr. Jenkinses called, "Your time is almost up."

"Progo! What will you do?"

Proginoskes folded its great wings completely about itself. All its eyes were covered. "*Not*. If you fail, I will not myself."

Meg swung around and faced the three men. "Mr. Jenkins Three—"

He stepped forward, smiling triumphantly.

She shook her head. "No. You are not the real Mr. Jenkins. I don't care how much tessering would shake him. He'd never make all

those promises." She looked at Mr. Jenkins One and Two. Her hands were ice-cold and she felt the feeling in the pit of her stomach which precedes acute nausea. "Mr. Jenkins Two—"

He stepped forward.

Again she shook her head. "You kept telling me to name you. Mr. Jenkins would never ask me anything. The only one of you who is as bad as the real Mr. Jenkins is Mr. Jenkins One—" Suddenly she gave a startled laugh. "And I do love you for it!" Then she burst into tears of nervousness and exhaustion. But she had no doubt that she was right.

The air was rent with a great howling and shrieking, and then a cold nothingness even emptier than the wrinkle in time of tessering. For a horrible moment she thought that she had been wrong and it was the cherubim being made not, but then she saw that there was only one Mr. Jenkins standing on the hilltop and that Proginoskes was still there, delicately unfolding wing after wing.

"Well, Meg—" Mr. Jenkins said.

"It's all right, Mr. Jenkins. I know you're glad you won't have to have me in school this year, and I don't blame you."

"Perhaps—" he started awkwardly, then said, "No. I doubt very much, Margaret, that there will ever be much understanding between you and me. And yet I feel a strange pride that you knew who I was. I feel—yes, I actually feel a certain affection for you. But it is just as well that we are not likely to meet again."

Meg found herself caught between two of Proginoskes's wings. "I'll take you to the dining hall, Meg, and we'll tell the others all about it. There's always a great storytelling banquet when anybody passes."

"Calvin and Mer-boy—Charles Wallace and Sporos—"

"They'll be there, and we'll find out about their adventures, too."

"Did they pass?"

"My dear Meg, as some earthling once said, that's another story. In fact, it's two more stories. I do know nobody failed today—we couldn't be having a banquet otherwise."

"Do cherubim eat?"

"Moderately, when we're mattered."

"I'm famished. And I'm—oh, Progo, wouldn't you like to feel? I feel absolutely glorious right now. Wouldn't you like to feel, too?"

Proginoskes stretched all its wings. Meg very clearly understood it to say, "I am doing the cherubic equivalent thereof." Laughter rippled through it. "Let's not worry about feeling. Joy is better. Come on, climb up, and I'll fly you to the banquet."

Meg clambered up, between wings and eyes, and seated herself in the cherubim. He rose swiftly into the shining air, and they flew rapidly past the hill and over the river and valley, leaving Mr. Jenkins staring after them, and calling, "Don't get any ideas, Margaret! Don't think just because I'm not around you won't have to work!"